# THE ZACK FILES

## Dr. Jekyll, Orthodontist

For Judith, and for the real Zack,
with love—D.G.

# THE ZACK FILES™

## Dr. Jekyll, Orthodontist

By Dan Greenburg

Illustrated by Jack E. Davis

GROSSET & DUNLAP • NEW YORK

I'd like to thank my editors,
Jane O'Connor and Judy Donnelly,
who make the process of writing and revising
so much fun, and without whom
these books would not exist.

I also want to thank
Jennifer Dussling and Laura Driscoll
for their terrific ideas.

Text copyright © 1997 by Dan Greenburg. Illustrations copyright © 1997 by Jack E. Davis. All rights reserved. Published by Grosset & Dunlap, a division of Penguin Putnam Books for Young Readers, New York. THE ZACK FILES is a trademark of The Putnam & Grosset Group. GROSSET & DUNLAP is a trademark of Grosset & Dunlap, Inc. Published simultaneously in Canada. Printed in the U.S.A.

*Library of Congress Cataloging-in-Publication Data*
Greenburg, Dan.
    Dr. Jekyll, orthodontist / by Dan Greenburg ; illustrated by Jack E. Davis.
      p.    cm. — (The Zack files)
    Summary: While Zack is being treated by Dr. Jekyll, his new orthodontist, the doctor undergoes a strange transformation into a growling monster.
    [1. Dentists—Fiction. 2. Horror stories.]    I. Davis, Jack E., ill. II. Title. III. Series: Greenburg, Dan.    Zack files.
PZ7.G8278Dr 1997
[Fic]—dc20
                                                                    96-38189
                                                                        CIP
                                                                        AC

ISBN    0-448-41338-8        C D E F G H I J

# Chapter 1

My name is Zack. I'm a pretty normal kid. But weird things happen to me all the time. If a weird thing has a choice of happening to me or to somebody else, it always picks me. I don't know why.

Like one time a ghost named Wanda trashed our apartment. Another time I got an electric shock in science class and for a while I could read everybody's mind. Also, about the best way to get to the parallel universe next to ours is through the medicine cabinet in my bathroom.

Well, you get the idea.

Anyway, you might not think that going to an orthodontist would lead to a weird and scary adventure. But you'd be wrong.

The time I want to tell you about started out normal enough. I went to the orthodontist because I had to have a baby tooth pulled.

I wasn't too thrilled about that. But my dad said we'd go for chocolate milkshakes afterward. So that was something. My mom and dad are divorced, by the way. I spend half the time with each of them. My dad is a writer, and he works at home. So he's the one who takes me to stuff like orthodontists and milkshakes.

Dad and I were sitting in the waiting

room. My old orthodontist, Dr. Silver, had retired. Now there was a new guy named Dr. Sheldon Jekyll. I knew because he sent me a card with a smiley face on it. It was the first smiley face I'd seen with teeth in it. Very straight teeth.

When I first heard Dr. Jekyll's name, I got a little spooked. There's this really scary book called *Dr. Jekyll and Mr. Hyde*. It's by Steven Louis Robertson. Or maybe it's Robert Louis Stevenson. Anyway, it's somebody like that. Maybe you've read it. It's about this nice doctor who turns into a monster named Edward Hyde. It happens every time he drinks some kind of potion.

I joked with my dad about it. He said it was just a made-up story. And things like that don't happen in real life. He always says stuff like that. But I know better.

While Dad and I were sitting in the waiting room I noticed this much older girl. She was about thirteen. I'm ten. She smiled at me. Boy, were her teeth straight! They reminded me of Dr. Jekyll's smiley-face card. I guess going to an orthodontist was really working for her.

Just then the nurse told me to go in.

"Do you want me to go in with you?" asked my dad.

"Uh, no," I said. "Why?"

"Well, in case you were scared about having your tooth out. Or because you haven't met Dr. Jekyll before."

"Oh," I said. I did sort of want Dad to come in with me. But I didn't want to look like a big baby in front of that girl. "I think I'd like to go in alone, Dad," I said.

"OK," said Dad. He gave me a squeeze.

I went in to meet Dr. Jekyll.

Well, Dr. Jekyll wasn't at all scary looking. He had black hair combed straight back. He seemed really jolly. And he had a big smile. I mean we're talking wall-to-wall teeth.

"Hello!" he said. "Glad to meet you, Zack. Glad to meet you. I'm sure we'll get along just fine. And I promise not to pull the wrong tooth. Ha, ha. That was a little joke."

I smiled weakly. Then we shook hands. His hand was sweaty. He seemed a little fidgety. Well, I was a little fidgety myself. But I was the one having the tooth pulled. I don't know what *his* excuse was.

"Well, well, sit down, Zack. Sit down," said Dr. Jekyll. He rubbed his hands together. Like he was eager to get to work.

"Right in that chair there. That's right. Let me look at that tooth now. Open wide. Open wider. Aha! Yes. I see the little devil. Ha, ha. We can't have you making Zack's grown-up tooth grow in crooked, now, can we? We're going to have to yank you out of there, you little devil, aren't we? Ha, ha."

OK. Calling my tooth a little devil was a tiny bit weird. Talking to a tooth *at all* was weird. I admit that. But otherwise, I thought he seemed pretty normal.

"Zack," said Dr. Jekyll, rubbing his hands some more, "I'm going to give you nitrous oxide. Do you know what that is?"

"Laughing gas?" I said.

"Exactly," he said. "Have you ever had nitrous oxide before?"

"No, sir," I said.

"Well, I think you'll like it," he said.

He placed a mask over my nose. A long tube connected it to a tank of gas on the floor. He turned it on. I heard a hissing sound.

At first I didn't feel anything. Then I began to get dizzy. And then my head seemed to get very light. Just like a helium balloon. I felt if I didn't hold on to it, my head would float right up to the ceiling.

I could see it. My head *was* a helium balloon. Floating on the ceiling. Suddenly that seemed the funniest thing I had ever thought of. I started to giggle. Dr. Jekyll giggled, too. I laughed hysterically. So did Dr. Jekyll.

Then he took a pair of pliers and pulled my tooth. I thought *that* was funny, too. Dr. Jekyll must have thought it was even funnier than I did. He was laughing so hard, his face got red. Then it got purple. Then his eyes sort of bulged out and got wild looking.

I thought he might be having a heart attack. And for some reason I thought that was funny, too. He started staggering around the office. He looked like one of the Three Stooges. I was laughing so hard I was almost choking.

Then—and I'm not sure about this—it seemed his hair grew longer. And his teeth were growing, too. Long and crooked. Like fangs. I was laughing so hard, I was gasping.

Dr. Jekyll wasn't laughing anymore. He was growling.

"Oh, no!" he shouted. "It's happening again! I can't believe it! I can't stop it! Aaarrrgghh! AAARRRGGHH!"

# Chapter 2

Dr. Jekyll kept staggering all over the office. His hair was wild and crazy looking. He started toward me, the pliers still in his hand. It looked like he was getting ready to pull another tooth. Oh, no!

"Help!" I shouted. "Get me out of here!"

But I was still laughing. It was the weirdest feeling I've ever had. Being scared to death and being unable to stop laughing.

Dr. Jekyll came closer. I couldn't move

my arms or legs. It felt like I was strapped into the chair.

All of a sudden Dr. Jekyll lurched to a stop.

"What am I doing?" he cried. "I must stop this."

He grabbed a bottle off a shelf. He tore off the top. He gulped it down.

A second later Dr. Jekyll stopped growling. He stopped staggering around. His hair lay back down on his head. His teeth grew back into his mouth. His face went from purple to red. Then from red to pink. He cleared his throat. He patted his hair. He looked nervously at me and smiled. Nice straight TV-ad teeth again.

He took the gas mask off my face.

"Well, now," he said. "How do we feel?"

"Uh, I can only speak for myself," I said.

"And how do *you* feel?"

"OK, I guess," I said.

I was telling a huge fib. I didn't really feel OK at all. I just said that in case Dr. Jekyll was getting ready to go berserk on me again. I was pretty shaken up, if you want to know the truth. My old orthodontist, Dr. Silver, hardly ever went berserk on me.

Dr. Jekyll was putting a wad of cotton into my mouth. Then he put the pulled tooth in a tiny blue plastic box that was supposed to look like a treasure chest.

"That little devil is right in here now, where he belongs," said Dr. Jekyll. He handed me the little plastic treasure chest.

The laughing gas had worn off by now. I started to wonder. Had I really seen what I thought I saw? Or was it just some kind of crazy dream? Maybe it was something the laughing gas did to me. But it had all seemed so real.

Dr. Jekyll handed me a little paper cup.

"What's this?" I asked.

"It's just mouthwash," he said. "Miracle Mouthwash. It's truly yummy. I invented it. Try it."

I tried it. It did taste pretty good. Sort of like bubble gum. And a little bit like peanut butter and chocolate. I swished some around in my mouth. I spit it out in the spit bowl.

"Don't spit!" shouted Dr. Jekyll. "DON'T SPIT!"

Uh-oh, I thought. Here we go again.

Then, in a much calmer voice, he said, "This is *special* mouthwash, Zack. It's all right to drink it."

"Really?" I said. I took another cup and

swallowed it down. "No dentist has ever told me I could drink mouthwash before."

"Well, Zack, I'm not like other dentists," he said.

Boy, you can say *that* again, I thought.

# Chapter
# 3

I waited till we were out of the office and in the coffee shop before I told Dad what happened. I looked around to make sure nobody could hear me.

"Dad, what would you say if I told you that when I was in Dr. Jekyll's office he turned into a monster?"

Dad chuckled.

"I'd say you had a great imagination," he said.

Dad was having a chocolate milkshake, too. Part of it was on his upper lip, like a mustache.

"Yeah, but that's what really happened," I said. "I think."

"What are you talking about?"

A man and woman sat down in a booth behind me. I leaned in close to Dad and whispered.

"Dad," I said, "right after Dr. Jekyll pulled my tooth, he started changing. His face turned purple. His hair grew wild. His teeth grew long and crooked. He started growling. And he said something about how it was happening again, and how he couldn't stop it."

Dad looked at me to see if I was putting him on. I wasn't.

"And then what?" he asked.

"And then he drank some stuff out of a bottle. And he calmed right down again," I said.

Dad was looking at me strangely. I slurped up some of my milkshake. It tasted really good. Even better than Dr. Jekyll's mouthwash.

"And this happened when?" Dad asked.

"Well...let's see. He gave me the laughing gas and..." I went no further.

Dad was nodding and smiling. He seemed relieved. He wiped his mouth with a napkin. No more mustache.

"You've never had nitrous oxide before, have you?" he said.

"No, but..."

"I think it was just the gas," he said. "First time and all."

Well, it was certainly possible.

"Maybe you're right," I said.

"I doubt you'll ever experience anything like that again," he said. "As long as you live."

Dad had no idea how wrong he was.

# Chapter 4

When I woke up the next morning my mouth hurt where my tooth was pulled. I went into the bathroom. I pulled my lip way down and peered into the mirror. The hole looked fine. But the teeth next to it looked funny. I thought they looked more crooked. But how could that be? Probably it was my imagination.

I didn't think about it until a few days later. I was watching TV and laughing pretty hard. Dad looked at me strangely.

"What is it?" I asked.

"Have you been wearing your retainer at night?" he asked.

"Sure," I said.

"Even when you're at Mom's apartment?"

"Of course," I said. "Why?"

"It just seemed to me your teeth were looking a little crooked," he said. "It's probably just my imagination."

"No, Dad," I said. "I think they're more crooked, too."

My teeth *felt* more crooked. The two big front ones most of all.

Two days later I was back at Dr. Jekyll's office for my follow-up visit. I was going to ask him about my teeth. Dad left me in the waiting room. He had some things to do. He said he'd be back in half an hour.

The same girl I saw before was there.

She was on her way out. She smiled at me again. Funny. Her teeth looked more crooked than they did the last time.

What was going on here?

The nurse went down the hall to Dr. Jekyll's office to help him with a patient. I was all alone in the waiting room.

I noticed the nurse had left the file cabinet open. It had all the kids' files in it. I knew that in my file there was this photo of me. It was taken before I got my retainer. My teeth were real crooked then. I was scared they were getting that way again.

I knew the files were private. But I really wanted to see that photo of me. Before I could stop myself, I walked over to the cabinet. I started looking through the folders.

I couldn't find mine. But I found some-

thing else. It was a file marked "Dr. Jekyll—Personal." I know what I did next was wrong. But I peeked inside. There was a big envelope. Inside was a diary. I read one of the pages.

"Day 13. The experiments continue to go well. But they must remain secret for now. No one has ever done this before."

Secret experiments! Yes! Dr. Jekyll was up to no good.

Just then I heard footsteps. Was the nurse coming back? I panicked. I closed the drawer. I went and slipped the diary into my book bag. Then I remembered the nurse had left the cabinet open. I raced back and opened it again.

The nurse came back into the waiting room. She looked at me.

"What are you doing in my file cabinet?" she said.

# Chapter 5

The nurse looked angry.

"Those files are private," she said.

"It's OK," I said. "I didn't see anything."

"What didn't you see?" she asked.

"Anything," I said. "Any diaries or anything else."

Probably that wasn't the smartest thing to say. But it was all I could think of.

Luckily the phone rang just then. The nurse picked it up. The voice on the other end of the line was so loud I could almost make out the words. The voice sounded really angry.

"No, no, Mrs. Fortensky," said the nurse. "Surely Whitney's teeth can't be getting *more* crooked."

There was more yelling from the angry voice.

"Yes, Mrs. Fortensky, I'm sure you have very good eyes," said the nurse.

There was more yelling.

"Of course the doctor can see Whitney this afternoon," said the nurse. "Come in at four o'clock."

So! Other kids were getting crooked teeth, too! I had to read that diary. Then I'd know what Dr. Jekyll was up to. But right now Dr. Jekyll was calling me into his office.

"So," said Dr. Jekyll. "How are you today, Zack?"

He was smiling like he had just eaten a canary or something.

"OK," I said.

"Any problems?"

He was rubbing his hands together like they were cold. He looked kind of antsy, too. Just like the last time.

He had me sit down in the dentist's chair.

"Nope," I said. "No problems, sir."

"Good," he said. "How did that gum heal where I pulled the tooth?"

"Fine," I said.

"Excellent," he said.

He looked inside my mouth.

"Your mouth looks great, Zack," he said.

"It does?" I said.

"Really, really great."

"You don't think my teeth are just a little more crooked than last time?"

"Oh, no," he said. "That can't be. Absolutely not. In fact, I think they're getting straighter. They *have* to be getting straighter. Much straighter. Why do you ask?"

"No reason," I said. I thought I'd better drop it. Dr. Jekyll was starting to get worked up.

Right after he was done examining me, he gave me a little paper cup.

"What's this?" I asked. "More Miracle Mouthwash?"

"That's right, Zack," he said in this kind of fake television-announcer voice. "Miracle Mouthwash. It's delicious and nutritious. And it builds strong teeth in twelve ways."

I took a sip. I swished it around in my mouth.

"Drink it up," he said in the same eager voice. "It's good—and so good *for* you."

I pretended to swallow.

"There now," he said. "Isn't that yum-dilly-icious?"

I nodded.

"Well, so long, Zack," said Dr. Jekyll, shaking my hand. "Come and see me again in a month."

I didn't say anything. I couldn't. My cheeks were full of mouthwash.

# Chapter 6

Dad was in the waiting room. The second we got outside, I spit the mouthwash out on the sidewalk.

"What was that?" Dad asked.

"Miracle Mouthwash," I said.

Dad looked at me and frowned.

"Dr. Jekyll wanted me to drink it," I explained. "I didn't think I should."

"I've never heard of a dentist telling a patient to drink mouthwash," Dad said.

"Neither have I," I said. "That's why I decided not to."

I started to tell Dad about the diary. Then I stopped. Dad was going to be mad. Better if he got mad at home. So I waited till we were back at the apartment. I wasn't sure how to start.

"Dad," I said, "when I was in the waiting room, I looked through Dr. Jekyll's file cabinet."

"What?" he said.

"I'm sure my teeth are getting more crooked," I went on. "So I wanted to find that photo of me before I started wearing my retainer. Just to check. Instead I found something else...Dr. Jekyll's diary. And...I took it."

"You *took* it?" he said. Dad sank down in his chair. "I can't believe you did that!"

He looked really upset.

"Dad," I said, "I can't believe I did it either. But I *have* to read this diary. I'm sure it will prove to you that Dr. Jekyll is weird. And up to no good."

I took the diary out of my book bag. I opened it and began to read:

"'The experiments continue to go well. The subjects seem to like the taste. I like it, too. In fact, I love it. I mean, I really love it. It's yum-dilly-icious.'"

"Yum-dilly-icious?" said my dad.

"He used that same word in the office today."

"Well, it's a pretty goofy word," said my dad. "But it doesn't make him a criminal. And it's no reason to swipe the man's diary."

That was true. Still, I was pretty sure Dr. Jekyll was doing weird stuff.

"Let me keep reading," I said. "'...My

Miracle Mouthwash will be every bit as wonderful as I suspected. Just think of it— a way to straighten teeth without braces! When the world hears about this, I shall become famous. Perhaps someone will even give me my own TV talk show.'"

"A way to straighten teeth without braces?" said my dad. "What a great idea!"

True again. But something was wrong. I had drunk some of his Miracle Mouthwash. And it sure wasn't making my teeth straighter.

"Let me read more," I said. "'...To be absolutely safe, I have developed Anti–Miracle Mouthwash. It can immediately reverse any side effects. In case anything ever goes wrong. Which it never will. But still.'"

"Dr. Jekyll wants to guard against side

effects," said my dad. "That sounds pretty responsible."

"Dad!" I said. "Whose side are you on here? OK, listen to this: 'Saw seventeen patients today. All had at least one dose of Miracle Mouthwash. Many complained their teeth were *more* crooked. But I know that can't be so. After all, my subjects in the back room are responding so well! My Miracle Mouthwash is transforming them just as I planned. And they no longer seem to mind being kept here.'"

I looked up at Dad in horror.

"Dad, *he's keeping people in the back room! Against their will!*"

"It doesn't say against their will," said Dad. But he didn't sound so sure anymore. "It just says they're being kept in the back room. There must be some perfectly good explanation."

"Like what?"

"I don't know," he said. "Maybe they're out-of-towners. And they can't afford a hotel. And he's doing them a favor by letting them stay there."

"I don't think so," I said. Then I read some more. "Take a look at this: 'I find I am loving the mouthwash more and more. I cannot seem to get enough of it. I just had some a minute ago, and already I... Oh, no! It's happening ag...'" I showed Dad the diary. "See. The writing gets all wobbly here. And then it just kind of dribbles off the page."

Dad took a close look.

"Zack," he said, "I admit this is a little strange."

"Yes! And I bet Dr. Jekyll was looking a little strange, too. Right after he wrote that."

I could just picture it. The fangs. The wild hair. The buggy eyes.

"Don't you get it?" I said. "Dr. Jekyll must have started turning into a monster again. Dad, I want to go back to his office tonight. After everybody has gone home."

"And do what?" he asked.

"See what's in that back room."

Dad thought this over. He shook his head.

"The only reason I'd go there tonight," he said, "would be to put that diary back before anybody knows you swiped it. I don't like what you did. Not at all."

I broke out in a big grin.

"You mean you'll actually go with me?" I said.

"Only to put back that diary," he said.

# Chapter 7

After dinner, Dad and I went back to Dr. Jekyll's office building. A guard asked us to sign his book. We had to print our names and the time we entered. Dad put down "Edward Hyde and son." Ha, ha! Then we went up in the elevator.

We were lucky. The cleaning people were just leaving Dr. Jekyll's office.

"Hold the door," said my dad. And they did.

"I'm Dr. Jekyll," said Dad. "I forgot something in my office."

Wow! Dad was getting good at this breaking-and-entering stuff!

As soon as the cleaning people were gone, I went right to the file cabinet. I opened the drawer and put back the diary.

"Now let's go," said my dad.

"No," I said. "First we have to see who's in that back room. If I don't, I'll never know for sure what's going on."

Dad looked at me hard. He had a frown on his face. Then he shrugged and nodded.

We went down the hall past the examining rooms. We turned left. And there it was. A door with a sign on it: BACK ROOM. We pushed it open.

Inside it was completely dark. From

somewhere we could hear the soft trickle of running water.

I tried to find a light switch, but couldn't. In the dark we could hear something else. The sound of living things.

At last I found the switch.

I turned on the lights.

Dad and I both gasped.

There were the subjects of Dr. Jekyll's experiments.

And...they weren't human!

# Chapter 8

Several pairs of large yellow eyes stared back at us. Their faces were covered with brown hair.

"Oh, no," said Dad softly. "They're..."

"...beavers," I said.

Yes, beavers. Three groups of beavers. Each group had built a beaver lodge in a pool of water with small trees around it.

"Very strange," said Dad.

I looked at him and smiled this big smile.

"I told you so," I said.

"Strange, but also not against the law," said Dad.

We closed the door behind us. We walked closer to the beavers. The first beaver lodge had a little sign on it: CONTROL GROUP. NO MIRACLE MOUTHWASH. The beavers in this group looked like normal beavers. With big buck teeth. They were swimming around in their tank. Putting finishing touches on their lodge. Busy as...OK, busy as beavers.

Their lodge looked like a normal beaver lodge. It was nicely built, with good sturdy branches. The ends were chewed off cleanly.

The sign on the second lodge said: TEST GROUP 1. MOUTHWASH FOR 3 WEEKS. The beavers in this group had much straighter teeth. They were swimming around, trying to build their lodge. But they were having trouble gnawing the branches.

Their lodge didn't look so hot. The ends of the branches were sort of shredded. The roof looked like it was ready to cave in.

The sign on the third lodge said: TEST GROUP 2. MOUTHWASH FOR 5 WEEKS. The beavers in this group had great teeth. But their lodge was pathetic. No self-respecting beaver would ever want to live in it.

One of the beavers with straight teeth swam over and gave me a smile. His teeth were perfect. But I felt sorry for him.

"Dad," I said. "Beavers were never meant to have straight teeth. It goes against all the laws of nature."

"Perhaps you're right," he said.

"I don't get it," I said. "I thought Miracle Mouthwash made teeth crooked. But with these beavers…"

I frowned. I scratched my head. And then it hit me!

"Dad!" I said. "I think I understand! The mouthwash works on animals, but not on people! That's why my teeth are getting crooked! And that girl in the waiting room—" I shuddered. "Who even *knows* what she looks like now!"

On a shelf at the end of the room was a row of bottles. I went and took a closer look at them. One bottle was labeled ANTI-MIRACLE MOUTHWASH.

"Look," I said. "I think this is the stuff that Dr. Jekyll drank after he turned into a monster. Remember the diary? I think this is what turns him back into his normal self."

"What if we fed it to the beavers?" Dad asked. "Do you think it might make their teeth turn back into normal beaver teeth again?"

"It's sure worth a try," I said.

Just then there was a terrible noise in the outer office. Things were crashing to the floor. Glass was breaking. Something large was bumping into walls. It sounded like there was an ape loose.

Before we could hide, the door to the back room burst open. It hit Dad in the head. Dad sank to the floor.

He was out cold!

And in the doorway stood Dr. Jekyll.

Dr. Jekyll's hair was standing straight out. His eyes were bulging and bloodshot...and he was looking straight at me!

# Chapter 9

"**M**OUTHWASH!" shouted Dr. Jekyll. "NEED MIRACLE MOUTHWASH! NONE AT HOME! NONE HERE! NEED MORE! NEED MORE NOW! AAARRRGGHH!"

"Hi there, Dr. Jekyll," I said, trying to sound normal. "And how are you this evening, sir?"

"MIRACLE MOUTHWASH!" roared Jekyll. "CAN'T FIND ANY! NEED IT! NEED IT NOW! AAARRRGGHH!"

"Dr. Jekyll," I said. "I know you mean well, but your mouthwash isn't working. Look at me. Look at you! I don't want to be mean, but you're a mess. Miracle Mouthwash may straighten teeth on beavers. But it does the opposite to humans. The thing is—"

"MOUTHWASH! NOW! NOW!"

It was no use trying to talk to Dr. Jekyll. He was running around the room like a madman. But I had a plan. I grabbed the bottle of Anti-Miracle Mouthwash. I slipped it into my pocket.

"Yoo hoo, Dr. Jekyll!" I called. "I know where we can find some mouthwash!"

"WHERE? WHERE MOUTHWASH? GIVE ME MOUTHWASH!"

"Follow me, sir," I said with a smile. I led the way down the hall.

"MOUTHWASH?"

"Right this way, sir," I said.

Dr. Jekyll followed me into his office.

"WHERE MOUTHWASH? HERE? NOT HERE! ALREADY LOOKED HERE!"

"I have it," I said. "Sit right down in this dentist's chair, sir. Just relax. And I'll give it to you."

Jekyll sat down in his dentist's chair. The moment he did, I grabbed the mask with the laughing gas. I clamped it down over his nose. I turned on the gas.

Right away the gas started hissing. And Dr. Jekyll started giggling.

"Good boy," I said. "Very good boy! And as soon as we're done, you can go to the toy bin and choose a little plastic dinosaur to take home with you."

I took the mask off Dr. Jekyll's face. He was laughing like a madman. I took out the bottle of Anti-Miracle Mouthwash.

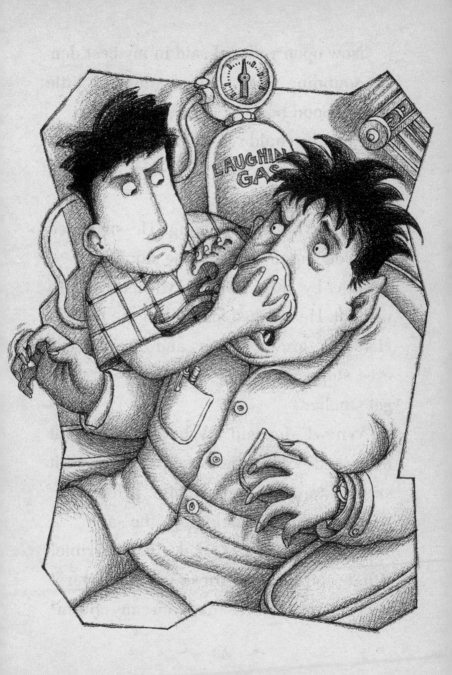

"Now open wide," I said in my best dentist-sounding voice. "Open wider. A little wider. Good boy!"

Before he could see what it was, I poured the whole bottle down Dr. Jekyll's throat.

Gulp! Down it went.

Dr. Jekyll kept laughing. He struggled for a few moments. Then he stopped.

Little by little, Dr. Jekyll returned to normal. He stopped foaming at the mouth. His hair grew shorter and neater. His eyes stopped bulging out. His crazy teeth got smaller.

"Whew!" he said. "Where am I? What happened?" Then he looked at me. And it seemed to come back to him. "Heh, heh, this is a little embarrassing," he said.

"Embarrassing?" I said. "It's horrible! What you did to those poor beavers! Beavers who never did you any harm!

Beavers are supposed to have buck teeth, not straight ones."

"But it's for the greater good," said Dr. Jekyll. "I'm going to straighten children's teeth without braces. With my Miracle Mouthwash."

"But it's not working on people!" I said. "Can't you get that through your head? Look at me! I'm starting to look like Bugs Bunny!"

Dr. Jekyll looked at me. Then he put his head in his hands.

"I never intended to hurt either kids or beavers," he said.

"Well, you have," I said.

"I guess man was not meant to tamper with the unknown," said Dr. Jekyll. "Man was not meant to drink mouthwash."

He looked up at me from the dentist's chair.

"Zack, I owe you a great deal," he said. "What can I do to repay you?"

"Give Anti–Miracle Mouthwash to all the kids," I said. "And give it to all the beavers. Promise never to drink Miracle Mouthwash again. Destroy any you have left."

"I promise," said Dr. Jekyll.

Just then Dad staggered in from the back room. He had a bump the size of an egg on his forehead.

"Dad, thank heavens you're OK!" I said.

"What happened?" Dad asked.

"Well," I said, "my patient here was having some problems. But we cleared them all up, didn't we?"

I looked at Dr. Jekyll. He nodded.

Once he was back to normal, Dr. Jekyll was as good as his word. He gave

Anti-Miracle Mouthwash to all the kids whose teeth had gotten crooked. Mine got straight again right away. So did the girl's in the waiting room.

The beavers were fine, too. The ones with straight teeth got big buck ones again. Dr. Jekyll donated all the beavers to the Bronx Zoo. I visit them there whenever I can. Their beaver lodges are so nice now, they could be in a magazine.

Because he was so grateful, Dr. Jekyll also promised me free dental work for the rest of my life. Dad was really glad about that.

And since then I never, never drink mouthwash at the dentist's office.

I don't think you should, either.

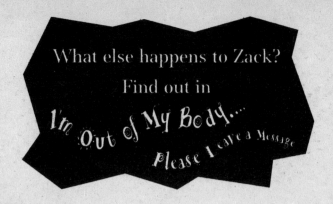

What else happens to Zack?
Find out in

I'm Out of My Body...

Please Leave a Message

And then, finally, I felt something. A little tickle against the hand on my bellybutton. "Seep out....Seep out," I kept telling my astral body.

A few minutes later I felt another tickle against my hand. This time it was like a breath. I opened my eyes. I was almost out of my body! But my leg was stuck. It felt like I was in quicksand. I pulled and pulled. Suddenly it popped free! And then I was floating in the air! Bobbing up against the ceiling!